STINK!

KATE & JIM McMULLAN

JOANNA COTLER BOOKS
An Imprint of HarperCollins Publishers

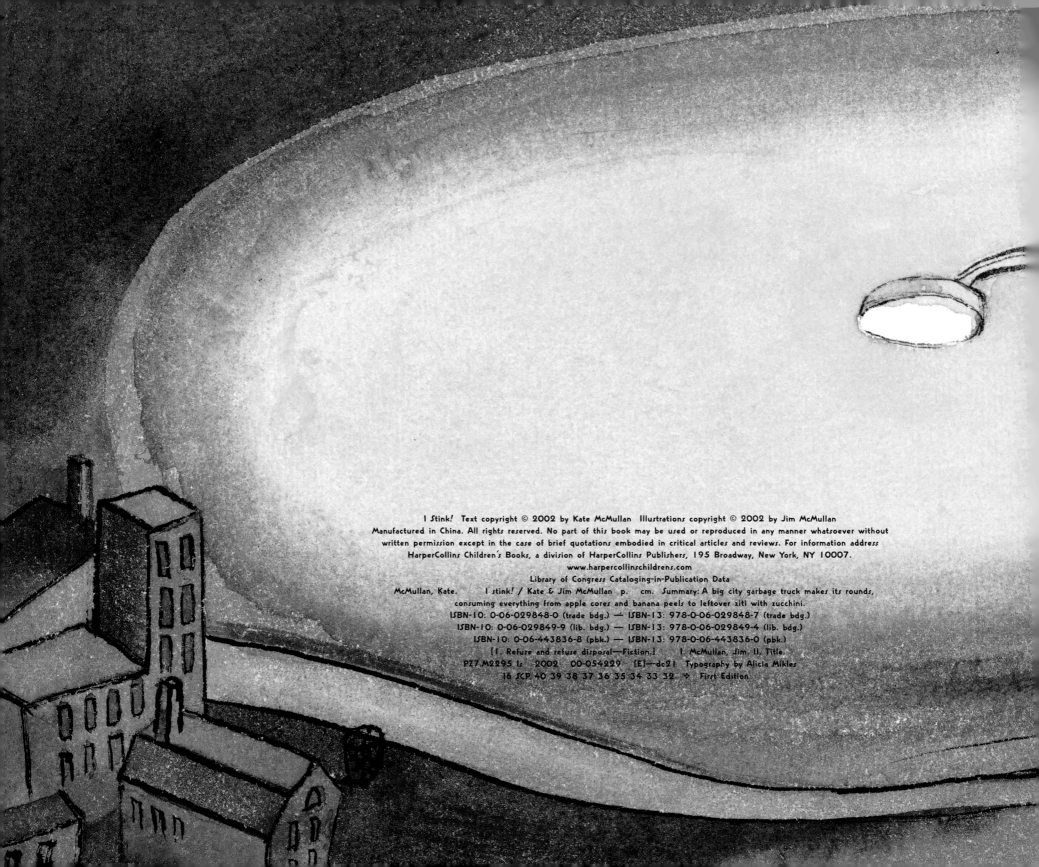

www.harpercollinschildrens.com
Library of Congress Cataloging-in-Publication Data
McMullan, Kate.   *I stink!* / Kate & Jim McMullan   p.   cm. Summary: A big city garbage truck makes its rounds,
consuming everything from apple cores and banana peels to leftover ziti with zucchini.
ISBN-10: 0-06-029848-0 (trade bdg.) — ISBN-13: 978-0-06-029848-7 (trade bdg.)
ISBN-10: 0-06-029849-9 (lib. bdg.) — ISBN-13: 978-0-06-029849-4 (lib. bdg.)
ISBN-10: 0-06-443836-8 (pbk.) — ISBN-13: 978-0-06-443836-0 (pbk.)
[1. Refuse and refuse disposal—Fiction.]   I. McMullan, Jim. II. Title.
PZ7.M2295 Is   2002   00-054229   [E]—dc21   Typography by Alicia Mikles
16 SCP 40 39 38 37 36 35 34 33 32 ❖ First Edition

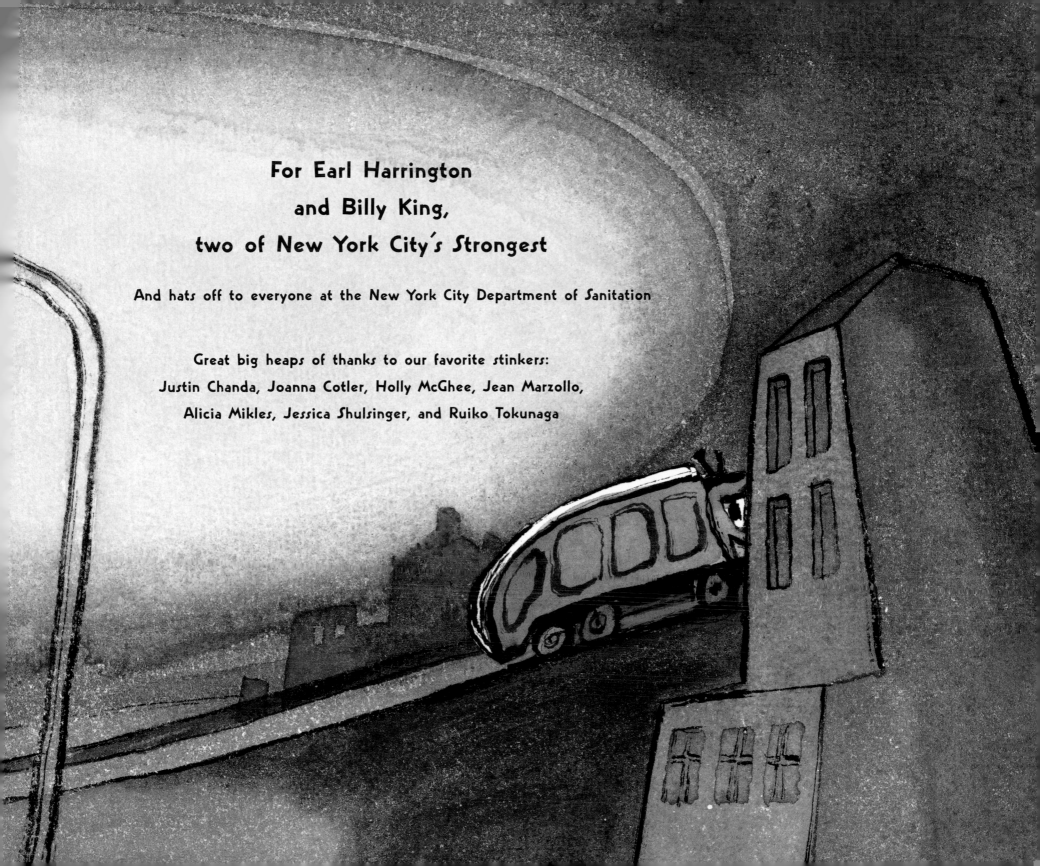

For Earl Harrington
and Billy King,
two of New York City's Strongest

And hats off to everyone at the New York City Department of Sanitation

Great big heaps of thanks to our favorite stinkers:
Justin Chanda, Joanna Cotler, Holly McGhee, Jean Marzollo,
Alicia Mikles, Jessica Shulsinger, and Ruiko Tokunaga

Who am I?
I've got lights.
Ten **WIDE** tires.
No A.C., not me.
I've got doubles:
steering wheels,
gas pedals,
brakes.
I am totally **DUAL OP.**
Know what I do at night
while you're asleep?

Feed me!

Straight into my HOPPER!

Nice toss, guys!

STOP!

Hopper's full.
Hit the **THROTTLE**.

Gimme some gas.
Rev me to the
MAX.

Engine?

ROAR!

Did I wake you?
Too bad!
PISTONS?
Bring on the crusher blade.
BLADE?
Push back the BAGS.
SQUEEZE them!
Crush them!
Mash them!
Smash them!
Whoa, those bags are
WAY
COMPACTED.

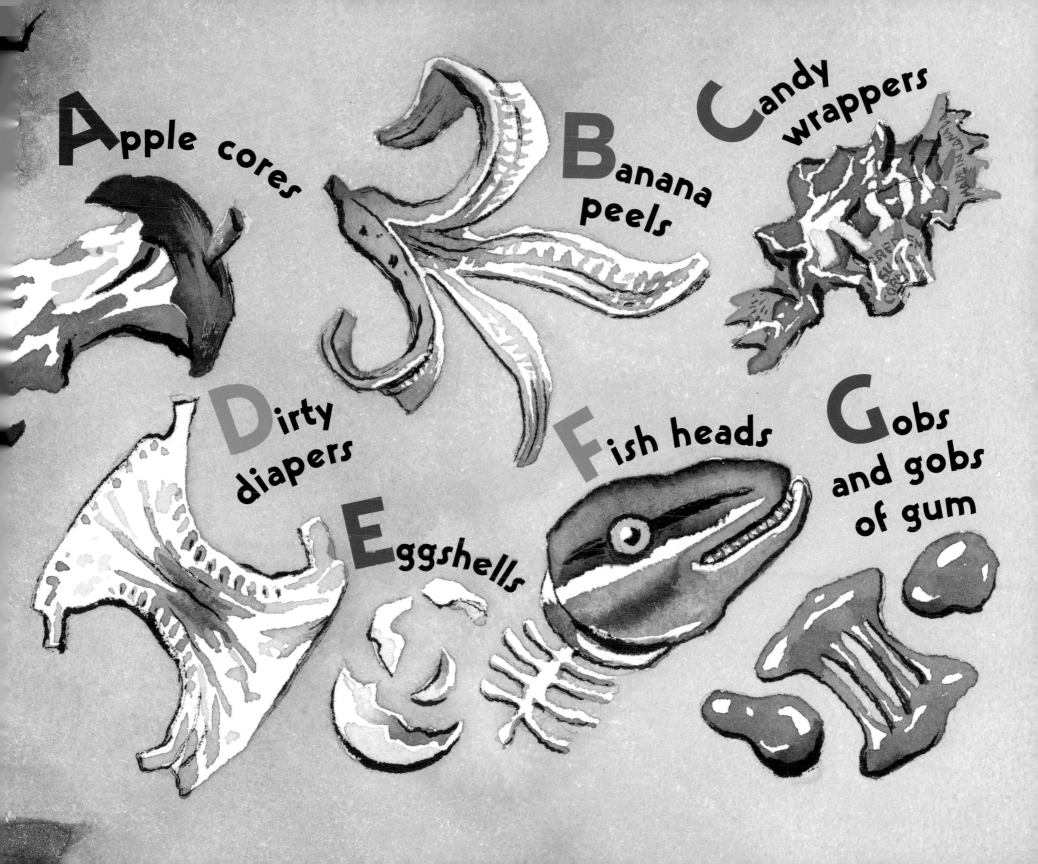

Apple cores

Banana peels

Candy wrappers

Dirty diapers

Eggshells

Fish heads

Gobs and gobs of gum

Half-eaten hot dogs

Icky ice cream cartons

Jam jars

Kitty litter

Lobster claws

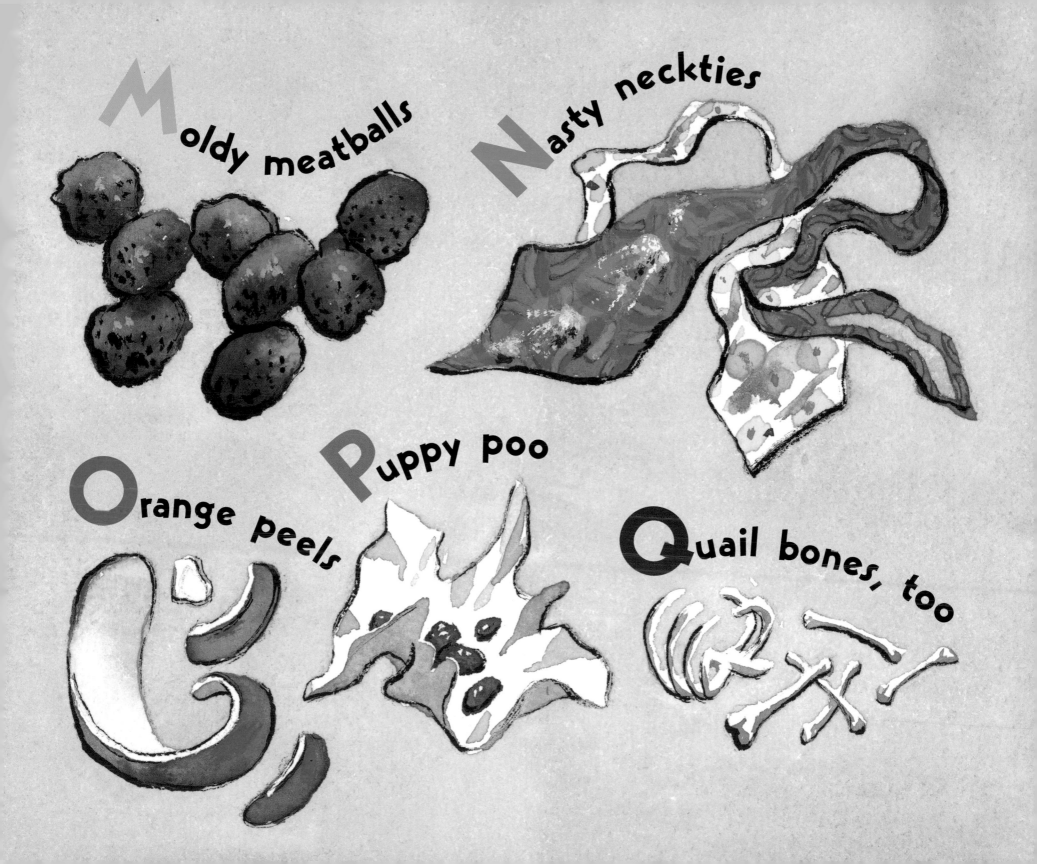

Moldy meatballs

Nasty neckties

Orange peels

Puppy poo

Quail bones, too

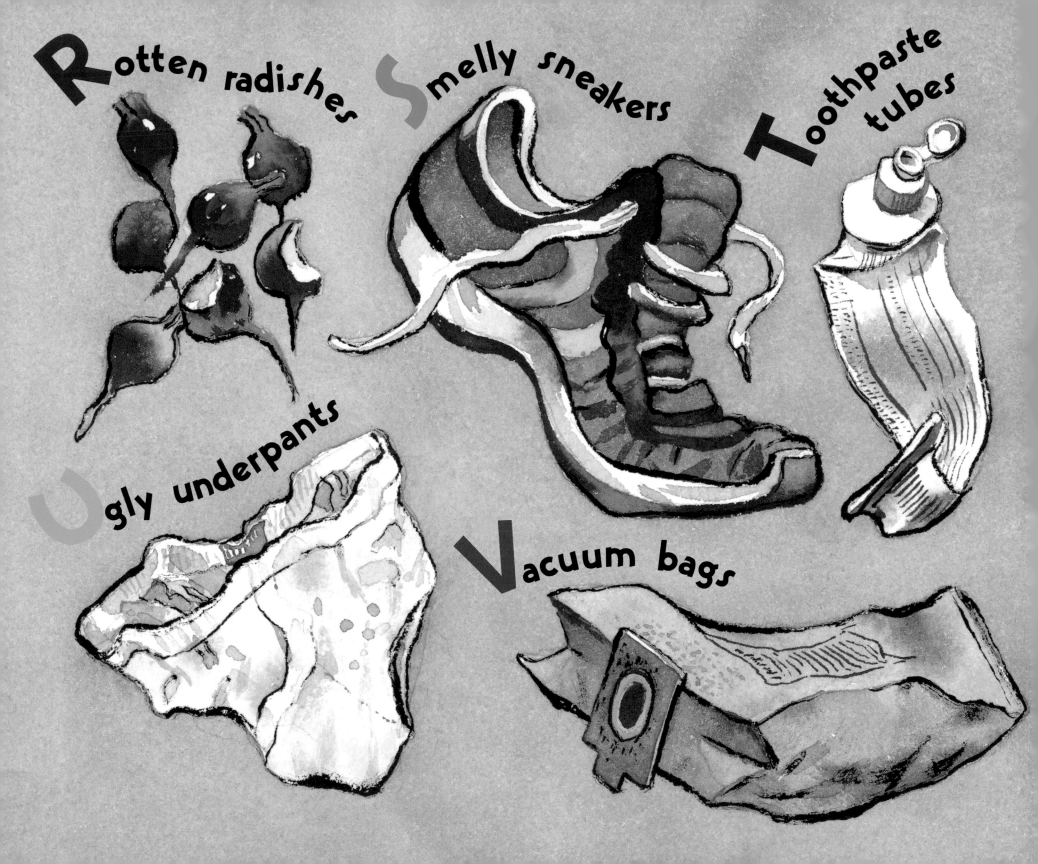

Rotten radishes **S**melly sneakers **T**oothpaste tubes

Ugly underpants **V**acuum bags

Next stop, the river.

Lights?
FLASH!
Driver?
REVERSE!

Get me to the barge.

Hear me blast my

BACK-UP Rap:

Ready, crew . . .
ACTION!

Pins?
OUT!

Power take-off switch?
HIT IT!

Tail gate?
SEPARATE!

Up, up, up!
Tail-gate sweeper?

EJECT!

PLOP!

I'm empty.
I'm beat.
You're waking up now,
but I need some Zzzzzzzzzzzzzzzzzzzz's.
Back to the garage crew.
Hose me down and gas me up.
See you tomorrow night, guys.

THAT'S WHO.